# Simone's Diary

*Dear Mr Cohen . . . Hi, it's me, Simone Anna Wibberley. Do you remember me from when you were a student on teaching practice with Miss Cassidy's class? . . . I am applying to be in your experiment . . . I will answer everything as fully as I can . . . I am quite good at this sort of thing because I used to fill in a lot of questionnaires in magazines with my dad's ex-girlfriend, Alexis . . .*

Simone has left Woodhill Primary School behind her and is starting life at her new secondary school. It's a little bit scary and there are lots of new things to get used to, so when she's asked to take part in an experiment by writing a diary and filling in questionnaires about her new experiences at Bartock High School, it's the perfect opportunity for Simone to write down all her thoughts and ideas in her own inimitable style.

Helena Pielichaty was born in Sweden to an English mother and Polish-Russian father. Her family moved to Yorkshire when Helena was five where she lived until qualifying as a teacher from Bretton Hall College in 1978. She has taught in various parts of the country including East Grinstead, Oxford, and Sheffield. Helena now lives with her husband, who is also half-Polish, in Nottinghamshire where she divides her time between looking after their two children, writing, teaching, and following the trials and tribulations of Huddersfield Town A.F.C. *Simone's Diary* is her fifth novel for Oxford University Press.

# Simone's Diary

Other books by Helena Pielichaty

# Simone's Diary

Helena Pielichaty

Illustrated by Sue Heap

OXFORD
UNIVERSITY PRESS

# OXFORD
UNIVERSITY PRESS

Great Clarendon Street, Oxford OX2 6DP

Oxford University Press is a department of the University of Oxford.
It furthers the University's objective of excellence in research, scholarship,
and education by publishing worldwide in

Oxford New York

Athens Auckland Bangkok Bogotá Beunos Aires Calcutta
Cape Town Chennai Dar es Salaam Delhi Florence Hong Kong Istanbul
Karachi Kuala Lumpur Madrid Melbourne Mexico City Mumbai
Nairobi Paris São Paulo Shanghai Singapore Taipei Tokyo Toronto Warsaw

with associated companies in Berlin Ibadan

Oxford is a registered trade mark of Oxford University Press
in the UK and in certain other countries

British Library Cataloguing in Publication Data available

ISBN 0–19–271842–8

3 5 7 9 10 8 6 4

Designed and typeset by Mike Brain Graphic Design Limited, Oxford

Printed in Great Britain
by Biddles Ltd, *www.biddles.co.uk*

# Wanted

**Bartock University: Educational Studies Department**

Are you in Year Six now but about to start Year Seven in September?

## I need your help!

I am researching for my MA into how pupils deal with the change from primary to secondary school.

It will involve completing simple questionnaires and a diary over the course of the year.

If you are interested please complete the permission slip below.

Yours gratefully,

*Ben Cohen*

Ben Cohen

✂------------------------------------------------------------------------

I/We give permission for: _____ to assist you in your research.

Signed: _____ (parent/guardian)

Fax: 01899-435600
e-mail: cohen@bartuni.co.uk

August 28th

To: Ben Cohen
Bartock University
Spire Lane
Bartock

Dear Mr Cohen,

Hi, it's me, Simone Anna Wibberley. Do you remember me from when you were a student on teaching practice with Miss Cassidy's class? I was the one with asthma who hung around with Chloe Shepherd. Chloe used to love you and write notes to you and get told off for bugging you when you were trying to put up display work. I don't hang out with Chloe much now—she's been away to Kids Camp in France for most of the summer. I see more of Melanie McCleod but Melanie's only a Year Five, nearly Six, not a Year Six nearly Seven like me, so I suppose when school starts I'll see more of Chloe again.

I am applying to be in your experiment. I think the questionnaire and diary idea is a good one. I hope it's not too late to take part but my mum only found the slip last night when she was tidying out my old school bag and saw it crumpled up with some book reviews and an empty packet of NikNaks. At first I couldn't work out how Year Sixes could help with your MA, because MA is American for 'Mum' but my 'ma' explained it meant Master of Arts. If you were a girl, would you get a Mistress of Arts? Mum doesn't mind me taking part but she hopes you will be enclosing stamps because it's going to be expensive posting the documents to you every two minutes, no offence, though she does understand what it's like to be a student because she is one herself. As well as cleaning five offices and two houses to make ends meet, she goes to Bartock College. She is training to be a physiotherapist which means she'll be useful to have around if you sprain anything or get stiff muscles.

Before we begin I'd better tell you that my mum and dad are divorced so you don't get confused or embarrassed. I live with my mum at the above address except every other weekend and Wednesdays when I'm at my dad's. The Wednesdays are an experiment, too, like your MA. Mum has late night lectures after cleaning The Bramley and Bridlington Building Society on Wednesdays from September so Dad has to start doing his fair share. Dad lives at The News Shack in Main Street, Bartock, if you need him for the father's opinion on anything.

I will answer everything as fully as I can because I know fullness is important. I am quite good at this sort of thing because I used to fill in a lot of questionnaires in magazines with my dad's ex-girlfriend, Alexis. The last one we did together was called: *Is it time to make up or break up?* Alexis got mostly C's, which meant it was time to break up, so she dumped my dad the day after. Dad was shocked and said he'll never be able to fathom women out and he's sworn never to look at another female as long as he lives. Mum snorted and said, 'Yeah, right,' when I told her but he's kept his word so far and it's been over three weeks. He's got a computer now instead. That reminds me.

Do you remember when you were a student at our school and you used to help Peter Bacon with his work because he had special needs but you always forgot to save the text and lost his stuff every time? I hope you are better at IT now. Let me know if you need any assistance as I am good at IT, though I'm even better at design and technology, but not in a big-headed sort of way.

Yours sincerely,

Simone Anna Wibberley

Chard Halls
**Bartock University Campus**
Bartock

Sept 2nd

Dear Mrs Wibberley and Simone,

Thank you for agreeing to take part in my research. I remember Simone very well from my time at Woodhill Primary so I'm confident that I'll have at least one reliable person filling in the details.

Find enclosed:

1. The first questionnaire for Simone.
2. The diary for Simone's first week at school.
3. Stamped addressed envelopes for their return (point taken!)

Yours sincerely,

*Ben Cohen*

Ben Cohen

# Questionnaire 1:
before starting secondary school

**Name:**

Simone Wibberley

# Questionnaire

Please answer as fully as possible. Thank you
**Date:** Sept 3rd

To be completed before you start secondary school

1. **How old are you?** 11 years and two months. I'll be the youngest in your experiment, probably.

2. **Are you male or female?** Female, thank you.

3. **Name of Primary School:** Woodhill Primary School (no motto)

4. **Name of Secondary School:** Bartock High School
(motto: Through learning comes joy)
My dad laughed when he saw the motto. He says the only joy he ever had at school was when the bell went at quarter to four. As for learning, he never learned a thing. Mum said, 'Nothing like stating the obvious.'

5. **How have you been prepared for secondary school?**
We have had loads of preparation. First, I looked round with my mum and Jem, her partner (she says she's too old to call him her boyfriend). You won't know this because my mum didn't start going out with him until after you had left, but do you remember when we went to see *Rumpelstiltskin's Revenge* at the theatre? Well, Jem was Rumpelstiltskin, though you probably know him best as the voice of 'Squeezy Cheese'. He's with Mayhem Theatre Company doing *Wind in the Willows* next month. If you are a theatre goer, or like animals, you might want to catch it. Tickets are cheaper on Wednesday afternoons, if you're impoverished.

Anyway, Mum and Jem thought the school had a nice atmosphere, even if it was a bit shabby. My favourite room was the CDT room, which was so cool. You should see all the equipment in there. I can't wait to get at the saws and stuff.

Then in July we had an Open Day and our class went with all the other Year Six classes from round here. We sampled a typical school lunch and met our form teacher. I'll be in 7DC with Mr Curbishley. Mr Curbishley has spiked up hair and did not wear a tie like the other men teachers. Chloe thought he was setting us a bad example because he sat on the edge of his desk when he talked to us. Jem said to take no notice because Mr Curbishley is probably a maverick and I need as many of them as I can get at school because they're often the best. Jem's maverick means '*an independent-minded person*', not the Maverick who was a fine cowboy like my dad said, or the Maverick chocolate bar, in case you get confused.

Jem teaches me a lot of new words except when he is rehearsing because he's Ratty! (Get it, 'ratty' like in *Wind in the Willows*. Sorry—Mum says I'm going to confuse you and to stick

15

to the question asked but I love writing to people and how are you going to understand my character if I don't tell you things and tell jokes now and again? I want you to get a level 4 in your MA. If you're very clever, can you do an extension paper like in the SATs?

Another thing the school did was that Mrs Warrener, the head of Year Seven, came in to talk to us but I missed that day because my hay fever was really awful. Everyone said she was nice though, even if she did have garlic breath.

To summarize, therefore, I feel I have been well prepared.

**6.   Was it the first school of your choice?**

Yes. The only other school is Alabaster Girls and I would have had to take an exam to get in there and Mum said she wouldn't want me to go through that pressure because life is hard enough and I agree.

Mrs Bent, my Year Six teacher, made her son Anthony go through it for Alabaster Boys and he passed which is good because he's a real bighead and I'm glad to be rid of him.

To summarize, therefore: yes, it was the first choice, though Mum wants to know if this is a political question, because if it is, she could write you a ten thousand word essay on the subject of parental choice but I told her you wouldn't have time to read it. Dad agreed with me; he says students only read *Viz* and the *Sun* anyway.

**7.   What do you know about the school already?**

It is huge and they serve Sunny Delight drink and flapjacks at break that cost 50p. The uniform is navy blue skirt or trousers, white polo shirt in summer or white shirt with gold and maroon tie in winter, maroon sweatshirt, and sensible black shoes (all year round). The worst bit of the uniform is sewing the name tags in—it took Mum and Jem and me ages. I did the ones in my Games socks.

What else do I know? There is a teacher there called Mr Skibereen who is supposed to be really, really, really strict and another one called Mrs Dinnington who has a withered arm but you mustn't stare. Anthony Bent says the older kids will flush my head down the bog because there is a lot of bullying at Bartock and the teachers drink alcohol during lessons but how does he know? Oh, and Melanie's big sister, Toni, who used to be at Bartock High but left to become a single mother, says the science corridor is haunted. It seems a funny place for a ghost. If I were a ghost I'd haunt somewhere decent, like a castle or a mean person's house.

**8. Are you looking forward to going?**
Yes, I am.

**9. List five things you are looking forward to the most.**

- Being treated like a grown up.
- There are lots more facilities and trips.
- Having a big choice of teachers means that they can't all have a son in their class who will be their favourite.
- The food is self-service and you have proper plates instead of babyish yellow trays, but you're not allowed only chips and chocolate cake every day. Peter Bacon was dead upset about this but I told him it's better for his health. He's going to have pizza and chips every other day instead.
- They have CDT rooms with masses of equipment like hegner-saws, so I'll be able to make decent inventions out of proper things instead of toilet rolls and string. And the CDT teacher will not confiscate glue guns from everybody like Mrs Bent did just because Peter Bacon and Freddie Jeffries once had a mock fight to see who was the quickest on the draw.

**10. List five things you are not looking forward to.**

- Getting lost on the first day because the school is so massive.
- Losing my bus pass and catching the wrong bus.
- If any naughty kids or bullies are in my class (just in case Anthony's right).

- What if I get a detention because the work is too hard and I can't do it and I fall behind? Especially maths. I only just scraped a level four in maths and still don't really know my eight times table.

- If Chloe is in a mardy on the first day and doesn't sit with me in class and I'll be on my own.

- What if I have an asthma attack? And what am I supposed to do with my inhaler because Mrs Bent always looked after mine but we go to millions of classrooms at high school, not just one. I suppose if I hadn't been away when Mrs Warrener came in I would have known the answer to this already but Mum says she'll write me a note to give in on the first day.

  That's six points. I hope this doesn't ruin your pie chart.

**11. Is there anything you will miss about being in Year Six?**

I'll miss some of the Year Fives, especially Melanie. I'll miss Miss Cassidy, though she's called Mrs Arundel now because she got married in summer. I sent her a card from my dad's shop and I bought her a set of sherry glasses for when she has guests. And I'll miss the Wildlife Garden because it was our year that started it from rubble and weeds and we got rid of the rubble.

**Thank you for taking time to complete this questionnaire. Part 2 (enclosed) needs to be filled in during your first week at secondary school and returned at the end of it.**

*Ben Cohen*

You are more than welcome. I thought your questions were clear and precise. Well done, Mr Cohen, I award you one sticker.

**Bartock University:**
Department of Education

# Pupil's Diary

Please write down your impressions of each day of your first week at secondary school. Include your thoughts and feelings wherever possible. Drawings are acceptable. Use extra sheets if you require them.

**Please return by: September 14**

B Cohen

> **Dear Mr Cohen,**
> **I hope you don't mind but I've started the diary**
> **the weekend before because I thought you'd be**
> **interested in the build-up. I've also decorated the**
> **cover, to make it more appealing to the eye.**
> **Simone**

## SUNDAY SEPTEMBER 5TH

I spent the morning getting everything ready for when I start at Bartock High on Tuesday. I put my uniform and other stuff out on my bed for inspection. I like everything except the bag which is specially designed to prevent doing your back in but isn't very fashionable. I wanted one from JJB Sports but Mum said I had to stick to the list and not rebel or give in to the designer label culture until I am at least fourteen. I can't wait until I'm fourteen because that's when I can have a boyfriend, have my ears pierced, and have a TV in my bedroom, as well as rebel.

It's not fair, though, because Melanie has had her ears pierced since she was four and they've only gone septic once and Chloe already has a TV in her bedroom as well as a midi-hi-fi and a Playstation. It's no use saying anything to my mum, though, because once she's made her mind up about something that's it. She doesn't eventually give in and say yes, like Chloe said her parents do if you ask often enough or throw things. I tried asking over and over when I wanted a *Now that's what I call Music 59* CD and nearly got grounded before I was anywhere near the throwing stage. Dad's even worse. He said I can't have a boyfriend until I'm thirty-two. Not that I want one. I'm not boy mad like Chloe. It's hard having strict parents sometimes but it's useful as well.

Then I put the uniform away and got out my bag. This already weighs a tonne because it contains:

- 🔥 My French/English dictionary (heavy)
- 🔥 One Games Kit (lumpy)
- 🔥 CDT apron (scratchy but light)
- 🔥 3 pencil cases

I have three pencil cases because I had one as a gift from Chloe's gran in Australia—it's wooden and was carved by Aborigines. The second one is from Mum and Jem. It's a blue canvas zip-up one and folds out into three parts, with pencils down one section, rubbers, sharpeners and stuff in the middle, and maths apparatus on  the left. The third one is from Dad. It's metal with a picture of a dolphin diving into the ocean on the lid. Inside is a special fountain pen which glows in the dark and a massive rubber that says 'for big mistakes' across the front. I'll have to use them all because I don't want to hurt anyone's feelings but I wish they had asked me first because I was quite happy with the Aborigine one and they could have saved money or bought me something different, like a decent stapler or a *Now that's what I call Music 59* CD.

After lunch (roast chicken, mashed potatoes, carrots, and spring cabbage followed by Toffee Viennetta ice cream) I went to Melanie's.

Mr McCleod, Melanie's dad, used to be a thief but he has changed his ways for good. He was writing his autobiography when I arrived. He's only got as far as the title, '*Every McCleod*

*Has Silver In His Lining'*. At least I think that's what it said. Mr McCleod's an interesting man but a terrible speller. I might ask Dad where he got my rubber from and buy one for him.

Melanie was quiet which is not like her one bit, and I asked her what was wrong and she said, 'Nothing', and I said, 'There is', and she said, 'OK, then, I'm worried that you won't bother with me when you get to the High school', and I said, 'Don't be a geek, 'course I will.' I didn't tell her Chloe had phoned to say she was back from camp and was coming to tea tomorrow. They hate each other and I always end up playing 'piggy-in-the-middle' with them, so they're best kept apart, like peanut butter and ketchup.

Then Toni arrived with Conan. He's going through the 'terrible twos' even though he's only one and a half and immediately started screaming the place down until Toni gave him a family-size bag of Star Mix. I asked Toni how Alexis was and she said, 'Oh, OK, considering her heart is broken.' 'Who broke it?' I asked and Toni said, 'Your dad, of course, who else?'

Apparently, Alexis didn't really want to dump Dad, she was just testing him, but Dad hasn't even tried to get her back and she'd rather die than call him first because a girl has her pride. Toni asked me to have a word with Dennis and I said I'd try but he has a computer now and it wouldn't be easy. She was about to say something else but Conan started choking on a jelly cola bottle and she had to turn him upside down.

The truth is, I quite like it at Dad's without Alexis because I get more time on my own with him but I do like Alexis and wouldn't want her to suffer. I wish she hadn't tested him and

broken her heart so near to me starting a new school, though.
I've got enough to worry about.

Jem picked me up from Melanie's. He'd had a busy day, too,
helping Spuddy, his friend, paint Toad Hall. Jem says it's good
fun being an actor and he couldn't imagine doing anything else
but it doesn't pay well unless you become famous like Matt
LeBlanc or Ken Barlow. When we got home, Mum was out at
Auntie Laura's so we watched television until she came back. It's
good watching television with Jem because he knows lots of the
actors and says things like; 'She's so stuck up she's unbelievable'
and 'He's so wooden he could play a park bench.' I hope if he
ever tests Mum she gets mostly A's or B's because I like having
him around and would hate it if they split up.

I had Bird's Eye potato waffles with Tesco Baked Beans for
supper and went to bed at 9.15p.m., quite full, and wrote this.

MONDAY, SEPTEMBER 6TH

I had my hair cut at 'Suzie's Salon' this morning. I always have
Christine because she's the best and listens and doesn't make
any sudden movements. She gave me a light trim and was just
beginning my french plait so I'd look grown-up for school when
Anthony Bent came in with his dad and plonked himself on the
chair right next to mine.

Anthony had Pauletta cutting his hair. Pauletta squints and is
bad with her nerves so her hands shake. It explains a lot about
Anthony's hair. 'I suppose you're a total wreck about tomorrow,
Wibberley,' Anthony muttered to me. I admitted I was, a bit, and
he said he wasn't nervous at all because the Michaelmas Term at
Alabaster Boys didn't start until next week. I asked him if he
was helping you with your experiment and he said he was but
only because he was bored and needed something to occupy
him. He said he has written so much already he is having his
replies spiral bound before he sends them to you, so if
something huge and fat comes through the post you'll know
what it is.

Just before Christine finished my plait Anthony leaned right across and said that he had heard the bullying problem at Bartock High had reached epidemic proportions and that all the school's budget had been used up on bandages and cotton wool for the dying and injured. He said if I got stabbed in the corridor by a Year Eight or Nine, not to pull the knife out but to leave it in until the paramedics arrived otherwise I could bring my vital organs out with it. I don't believe him one bit but I could have done without his comments.

Chloe came in the afternoon and she was in a really good mood. She said Kids Camp had been brilliant because there were loads of boys there but was really serious about one called William. He was thirteen and a Taurus and they had kissed on the lips. She went on about William most of the time and didn't really want to discuss our plans for tomorrow, except to tell me not to bother saving her a place on the bus because her mother, Mrs Shepherd, is bringing her to school in her Cherokee instead. Chloe is not helping you with your survey. She says you can't get involved in such things and go through puberty at the same time.

Her mum and dad have bought her a mobile phone and a lap-top computer for school, in case you're doing a pie chart on gifts. She asked me what I'd got and I showed her my pencil cases. She said, 'Oh, never mind, it's the thought that counts.'

When she'd gone Mum and Jem took me to the cinema to take my mind off tomorrow but it didn't work. I still can't sleep now, and it's ten o'clock.

**11.30p.m.** Have had some warm milk and a ginger biscuit and Mum has been in and stroked my hair. I told Mum I was worried because I feel too old for juniors and too young for secondary. She smiled and said I was at sixes and sevens in more ways than one which didn't help much, even after the explanation.

**2.00a.m.** Still can't sleep. I'm trying and trying but I am too nervous about tomorrow. Maybe you could do a bar chart on 'average time high school children went to sleep the night before they started school'. I would come under the 'between 2.00 and 4.00 in the morning' category.

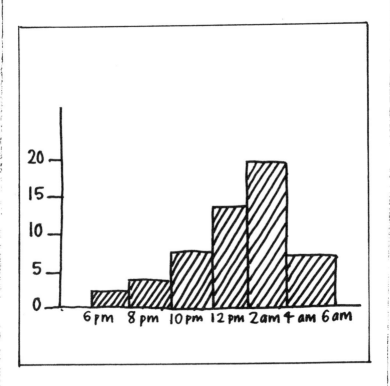

Dear Mr Cohen,

I hope you don't mind but I've written a lot today so I have split it up into 'before', 'during', and 'after'. I hope this doesn't thwart your database.

TUESDAY, SEPTEMBER 7TH

# Before

I was dressed by 6.00a.m. Then I was bored waiting for Mum to get up so I phoned Dad because I knew he'd be doing the papers and he said he'd just been thinking about me. He asked me if I'd packed my pencil case and I said I had and he told me if any kids gave me any hassle he'd be down the school like a shot, then he had to go because the Wynne twins hadn't turned up to do their delivery again and he had to sort it out. I felt a bit sad when he hung up. Phone calls are all right but they're not the same as a hug. I think even divorced people who have nothing left in common should get together on special occasions, like Christmas morning and their only child's first day at secondary school.

Then Mum and Jem got up and made a big fuss and I felt a bit better. Jem cooked his special Cakebread Pancakes which are really thick with masses of golden treacle dripping off the edges while Mum took about three million photographs of me. She was nearly crying and saying, 'How can my little baby be going to secondary school already? I can't believe it.' Then the post arrived and there were two letters for me. One was a card from Mel with a friendship bracelet inside and one was a card from Alexis. I wanted to wear Mel's bracelet but I daren't because bracelets weren't on the uniform list. It says so in the handbook, very clearly:

## N  O    J  E  W  E  L  L  E  R  Y
**may be worn except one small sleeper per ear.**
**Anything else will be confiscated.**

Mum sniffed at Alexis's card, which had a picture of a puppy on the front and said 'Thinking of you'. Mum said, 'That'll be a challenge for her,' and Jem laughed but I didn't think it was funny. I know Alexis helped to split Mum and Dad up but that was nearly four years ago and there's no need for sarcasm.

Then it was time for the bus. Mum wanted to come to the stop with me but I said no way and her bottom lip trembled so I gave her a long hug and said I'd be OK and she said, 'Yes, but I don't think I will.'

My stomach started churning as soon as I saw the Bartock High kids at the bus stop. There weren't that many because the Year Eights and Nines don't start until tomorrow, so at least I knew I wouldn't be stabbed. No one said anything to me. They weren't friendly but they weren't unfriendly. I wondered where Peter was because he only lives three doors up but then the bus came and I got nervous again because my photo was horrid on my bus pass and I was scared the driver might laugh but she hardly glanced at it. Peter jumped on just as the bus was about to leave. The driver did stare at Peter's pass then she laughed out loud. Peter's face went bright red and he said something but she just waved her hand for him to sit down and kept laughing.

I asked Peter why she was laughing and he said it was because of the accident. His dog, Beast, had slavered on his photo, so Pete had wiped it clean with the dishcloth but the dishcloth had been in industrial bleach and his face came off with the slaver, so Pete had tried to draw his face back on with a felt tip and it had gone wrong. He wouldn't show me it, though, so I don't know how wrong.

It took 45 minutes to get to school which is a long time. It might have taken less time if the driver hadn't kept looking round and laughing at us every two minutes. When we got off she told Peter he'd have to get a new photo put on, in case of inspectors, though as far as she was concerned it was OK because it was a good start to her day.

Her name was Hazel, by the way.

## During

All the Year Sevens had to go straight to the hall and sit in our form groups. Mr Curbishley, the maverick, was at the front. Chloe was already there and had saved us a place next to her on the floor. Mrs Warrener, the head of Year Seven with the garlic breath, was standing at the front. It was the first time I had seen her. She looked kind but firm, like Rita in *Coronation Street*, though not as old. She welcomed us to the school and said she hoped we'd all settle quickly and be happy and if we had any problems we had to see her and we weren't to worry about getting lost because the Year Elevens had been strategically placed to help us. I wanted to ask her about the rule on inhalers because Mum hadn't written the note but I daren't. Then Mrs Warrener told us we would be spending all morning with our form tutors and we would be dismissed one group at a time. We all got up but then she made us sit down again because we were too noisy. It took three goes before we were allowed to filter out, which is the same number as during assemblies at Woodhill.

Our class, 7DC, were last out because we were at the front. Mr Curbishley said, 'Come on then, troops, let's be having you,' and led us to a mobile classroom, Room 17, behind the science block. We were allowed to sit anywhere so Chloe and I sat at the back with Peter just in front of us. We're the only three in 7DC from Woodhill. I don't know where the rest were from but they seemed all right. A boy sat next to Peter but didn't say anything.

Mr Curbishley sat on the edge of the desk and gave us a big grin and said 'OK, let's get the boring bit over and done with', and we spent the whole morning going over the Code of Conduct and the timetable and rules and how to fill in our planners. Our planners are very important. We have to write in all our homework and any letters home and have them signed by our parents every Friday. If you don't have it signed you're in big trouble.

Here is a copy of my timetable and list of teachers for your research. I hope you find them useful. You could put them in your appendix. I mean the appendix Jem told me you would probably be putting at the back of your MA, not the one that can burst inside you and stick to your other bits.

# Timetable: Simone Wibberley 7DC

|  | Period 1 | Period 2 | Period 3 | Period 4 | Period 5 | Period 6 |
|---|---|---|---|---|---|---|
| **Mon** | Maths<br><br>KR<br><br>M1 | Drama<br><br>JW<br><br>D1 | Mod Lan<br><br>JE<br><br>Rm 6 | Art<br><br>LR<br><br>A2 | Science<br><br>DC<br><br>Lab 2 | Science<br><br>DC<br><br>Lab 2 |
| **Tues** | English<br><br>MP<br><br>E5 | PSRE<br><br>DC<br><br>R17 | Science<br><br>DC<br><br>Lab 2 | Science<br><br>DC<br><br>Lab 2 | Maths<br><br>KR<br><br>M1 | Mod Lan<br><br>JE<br><br>Rm 6 |
| **Wed** | Geog<br><br>AF<br><br>G3 | IT<br><br>LB<br><br>CR2 | English<br><br>MP<br><br>E5 | Music<br><br>PN<br><br>Mu 1 | Art<br><br>LR<br><br>A2 | Mod Lan<br><br>JE<br><br>Rm 6 |
| **Thurs** | CDT<br><br>LK/TOC/PK<br><br>Tech blk | CDT<br><br>LK/TOC/PK<br><br>Tech blk | English<br><br>MP<br><br>E5 | History<br><br>SS<br><br>Rm12 | Geog<br><br>AF<br><br>G3 | English<br><br>MP<br><br>Library |
| **Fri** | History<br><br>SS<br><br>Rm 12 | English<br><br>MP<br><br>E5 | Maths<br><br>KR<br><br>M1 | Maths<br><br>KR<br><br>M1 | Phys Ed<br><br>GG/GW<br><br>Sports H | Phys Ed<br><br>GG/GW<br><br>Sports H |

| Subject | Teacher |
| --- | --- |
| Head of Year | Mrs Warrener |
| Form Tutor | Mr Curbishley |
| English | Mr Pikelet |
| Maths | Mrs Ruskin |
| Science | Mr Curbishley |
| French | Mr English |
| German/Spanish | not until Y8 |
| Geography | Miss Fintz |
| History | Mr Skibereen |
| IT | Miss Brighton |
| P.E. | Mrs Gallon |
| PSRE/General Studies | Mr Curbishley |
| Art | Miss Rimmington |
| Technology | Mrs Kidner or Mr Kidner |
|  | or Mr O'Connell |
| Music | Mr Nixon |
| Drama | Mr Welch |

I can't believe I have fourteen different teachers. I'll never remember them all. And we have the really strict Mr Skibereen for history, so I'm not looking forward to period four on a Thursday and period one on a Friday. Lessons are called periods here. Chloe started giggling when Mr Curbishley said we would be having thirty periods a week. She said in a dead loud whisper that she thought one a month was bad enough (as if she knows) and I was scared in case anyone heard her but no one had.

I will get you a sample page of my planner when I go to my dad's tomorrow. He has a photocopier in his shop now. It costs 10p a go but is more trouble than it's worth.

Anyway, back to school. At break, Chloe and I wandered round the tennis courts, finding other kids from our old class and talking to them. I would have liked to get a flapjack but the queue was massive and that's without the Year Eights and Nines. I may never get to chew a school flapjack, ever.

After break, we had PSRE. We had to swap seats and sit with someone we didn't know unless we were doing that already. Peter and his partner stayed where they were and Chloe and me swapped with two girls across from us.

Then Mr Curbishley said we had to take turns to tell each other as much about ourselves as we could in two minutes. My partner was called Josephine Lyons. She lives on the new estate and plays about a million musical instruments even if she does bite her nails. When the time was up Mr Curbishley went round the class asking us to tell everyone what we had found out. I think Mr Curbishley just wanted us to mix because that's what you have to learn to do at secondary but it was hard remembering about Josephine and listening to all the others at the same time, especially when you are nearly last. When it was our row's turn, Peter's partner wouldn't say anything so

Mr Curbishley said he'd come back to him but just as he was walking past the boy leaned over and threw up right across Mr Curbishley's shoes. Mr Curbishley didn't shout or anything. He just said, 'Nice shot' and we all laughed to break the tension. Peter went with the  boy to the toilets to get cleaned up and Mr Curbishley had to telephone for the site manager to put some sand down. I felt sorry for the boy because it could have happened to any of us. Mr Curbishley leaned over and asked Chloe and me to keep an eye on Clifford (that was the boy's name). We said we would but I could tell Chloe didn't really want to. She's not very good with blood or vomit.

Lunch was brilliant. Miles better than at Woodhill. I had jacket potato, cheese and salad, chocolate sponge and custard, and a small carton of English apple juice. Mum told me I had to choose healthy options because of my asthma. Chloe had the same as me, even though she doesn't have asthma. Peter had just chips because he'd only brought fifty p. and didn't want me to lend him any. Clifford had fish fingers and chips and peas and two bottles of Sunny Delight. He didn't ask the serving lady for them, he just pointed. When we sat down he slid one of the bottles of Sunny Delight to Peter but still didn't say anything. He didn't speak the whole time. He must be very shy.

Are you doing a big section on food in your research? If you are, I could send you some typical menu prices. You could put your findings on food in a pie chart (pie chart, get it?)

After lunch was maths with Mrs Ruskin. Remember I was worried about maths because it is my weak area? Luckily we just had to copy out 3D shapes and colour them in and label them. I was quite pleased with my triangular prism. It helps that my mum eats a lot of Toblerones and I save the cartons for making things. At the end, though, just as I was feeling relaxed, Mrs Ruskin gave us homework. It's a mathematical investigation. This is it:

**Well, well, well**
**A person goes to a well with two jars, one of which**
**holds three pints and the other five pints. How can we**
**bring back exactly four pints?**

We have to ask two other people to do it, too, to see different ways of problem solving. It has to be in on Friday. I know I'll bodge it up. You wouldn't use jars in a well anyway, would you? You'd use a plastic bucket.

After maths was French with Mr English. When he told us his name he said 'don't laugh' but I don't think anybody was going to anyway.

He said he was new to Bartock High just like us. He looked very nervous. Chloe put her hand up and said she had been to France all summer and had a note asking if she could be given harder work than the rest of us. That made Mr English look even more nervous, especially after he had read the note. All we did was copy out a list of rules for doing neat work. Homework is to back our exercise book. At least I know I won't mess up on that.

# After

I sat next to Peter on the bus home. Hazel winked at us when we
got on and asked if we'd had a nice day. Peter went a bit red
again when he showed her his bus pass but she didn't make fun
this time. I think she was distracted by Mrs Shepherd, Chloe's
mum, blocking the bus lane in her Cherokee. Hazel called Mrs
Shepherd a few bad names and pipped her horn. I sat down
quickly because I know what Mrs Shepherd's like but luckily
Mrs Shepherd drove off before there was a nasty scene.

I asked Peter what he thought of Clifford and he said he
thought he was OK, except for the puking. I said at least he'd
made a new friend.

When I got in my mum just about cuddled me to death and I
had to tell her every single thing I'd done. I showed her the
homework and she scowled and said 'Oh, heck' and spent ages
in the recycling box finding two jars the same size. Anyway, that
didn't work because none of the jars was big enough so she kept
drawing jars and scribbling out saying 'I know the answer, I just
can't explain it.' She is not a mathematical thinker. That's where I
get it from. She said I ought to get Jem to do it because he was
good at maths but he was at Toad Hall. Besides, I want Dad to
do it but I didn't tell Mum that. I hope we don't get too much
homework where the grown-ups join in or it's going to cause a
lot of problems for kids whose parents are divorced. You could
do a survey on that, too.

I phoned Mel for a chat and to thank her for her bracelet and to invite her to watch a rehearsal for *Wind in the Willows* on Friday. She said she'd come if she wasn't babysitting. Mel said Mrs Bent was as mardy as ever and had made her miss break just for getting an answer wrong in Literacy Hour. She had to use a metaphor in context and said, 'I met her for a pint of cider.' I don't think you should miss break for that, do you? Not on your first day back when your brain's had a rest.

I told her about Clifford throwing up over Mr Curbishley's shoes and she said, 'Not Clifford Hammond?' but I didn't know his last name. If it is Clifford Hammond he lives near them and his family are dead hard and scare everybody. I said I didn't think it could be because the 7DC Clifford is shy. Then she asked me who I had sat next to and I told her 'Chloe' and she just said 'oh' and left it at that.

Mel gave her first day as a Year Six minus 500 out of 10. I give my first day at Bartock High

9/10

I have underlined all the key words for you to help you with your skim reading, Mr Cohen

## WEDNESDAY, SEPTEMBER 8TH

The bus was fuller this morning so Hazel didn't have time to laugh at Peter's photo. Peter's brother, Luther, who's a Year Nine, sat behind us with his friends and started messing up Peter's hair and teasing him about me, saying stuff like 'Sitting with your birdie, Peabrain? How sweet,' but we ignored them and they soon got bored.

It was straight into lessons today and we had <u>Geography</u> with Miss Fintz first. All we did was write out the rules of presentation and colour in a map of the world. The lesson was all right but not exactly exciting.

After break was <u>IT</u>. The IT block is brand new and we had a computer to ourselves instead of having to share. Miss Brighton, the IT teacher, spits a lot when she talks. She told us about Computer Club at lunchtimes and then we had to think of a password to use to get into our computers.

This is mine but don't tell anyone:

# ratty

At breaktime Chloe and I tried to queue up at the breakfast bar for a flapjack but it was no use. It was bad enough yesterday but the Year Eights and Nines just push in and call us little ****s. I can see why the teachers didn't let them in yesterday. It would have put us all off coming again. Chloe said she's going to tell her mum about it.

English with Mr Pikelet was excellent. He read out poems that made us laugh and then read out an extract from a story that made us sad and then he read out bits from a play that we didn't understand but made us feel scared then he told us a joke about an ape in a pub that made us laugh again and then he said, 'Aren't words sublime?' It was the quickest lesson I've ever had. I think Mr Pikelet might be a maverick, too. For homework we had to make a list of words that make us angry or happy. I'm going to do that then ask Jem what 'sublime' means.

Music was a bit messy to start with. Some people left to have private tuition, including Josephine and Chloe. Chloe's learning the violin because her mother thinks the ability to play an instrument is a sign of refinement. I made up a three at the keyboards with Peter and Clifford but just as we were about to start a man with an orange shirt and Star Wars tie interrupted and asked for Peter Bacon and Clifford Hammond. Then he grinned at the music teacher, Mr Nixon and said, 'You get Lennon and McCartney and I get Ham and Bacon!' I'm beginning to think teachers' jokes at high school are worse than my dad's, and that's saying something.

At lunchtime the Year Sevens were first so we didn't have to worry about being pushed to the back of the queue by the Year Eights and Nines. Josephine Lyons and her friend Tamla Kershaw sat with us. Tamla hadn't come yesterday because Mrs Warrener had said she'd have to take her nose stud out and she didn't want to but she'd given in today because otherwise she'd fall behind and she needed qualifications to become a journalist like her mother and her mother's mother before her. It's hard to concentrate on macaroni cheese when there's a girl opposite you with a small hole in her nose, even if the girl is ambitious.

After lunch was <u>Art</u> with Miss Rimmington. She is very pretty but I can't judge her ability as an art teacher yet because the keys to the store cupboard were missing so we just had a chat.

Last of all we had <u>French</u> with Mr English. We wrote down how to greet people. <u>Bonjour</u> is 'good morning' and 'good day', <u>Bonsoir</u> is 'goodnight', and <u>Salut</u> is 'hello'. I would have enjoyed French more if Chloe hadn't kept whispering, 'This is so easy.'

I give school 8/10 today and 6 of those 8 were for the English lesson.

After school I went to see Dad. I didn't sleep over because Mum thinks I should keep my first week of school simple and her course doesn't start yet so I just went for tea. I showed Dad the maths homework and he just put the answer in dead quick without any working out and said he wished you *could* get jars that carried three pints because it would save him going to the bar every two minutes. I wish he'd take things a bit more seriously, like your child's maths homework and alcoholic poisoning.

He did say that I looked grown up in my uniform and to remember what he'd told me about not going out with boys until I was thirty-two. I ignored him because you have to when dads tease their daughters. I showed him my timetable and list of teachers and he said he wouldn't mind meeting Miss Brighton but it put him off when I told him about the spit. I did a <u>photocopy</u> of this week's diary in my planner but I'm going to put it at the end so I can add anything that happens on Thursday or Friday. I hope that's OK. Dad didn't charge for it, by the way, but I mustn't make a habit of it because machines don't run on fresh air.

There was a bit of <u>tension</u> when Jem picked me up. Usually

Mum does it but Jem was passing on his way back from the theatre anyway so it made sense. Dad didn't invite Jem in when he called round the back. He made him wait next to the bundles of left-over newspapers. My mum was the same when Alexis used to pick me up for weekends, except without the newspapers. I'd be *so* told off if I left people standing in the cold at night time but the rules seem to be different for your parents' girlfriends and partners. Somebody ought to give them some tips on behaviour. Maybe you could do something like that for your next MA. It would be useful for everyone.

Oh no! I've just looked at my timetable and remembered I've got Mr Skibereen for history tomorrow. Help. At least I start off with the best subject in the world—design and technology. I wonder if we'll be allowed to use power tools straight away or if we'll have to wait until lesson 2.

41

## THURSDAY SEPTEMBER 9TH

I don't feel like writing today, Mr Cohen, sorry. It has nothing to do with Mr Skibereen, though.

## FRIDAY SEPTEMBER 10TH

Sorry about yesterday, Mr Cohen. I'd had a really bad day with Chloe and today wasn't much better but I've just had a long talk to my mum about it and I feel OK again and fit to write. I hope it doesn't mess up your 'Thursday' graph.

**Tip:**
All this next bit would probably go under '<u>friendship groups</u>' in your survey, Mr Cohen, not '<u>learning</u>'. And I think you should have this at the front, not in your appendix, because if kids have trouble with their friendship groups it stops them learning anyway. That's my opinion, and I am speaking from experience.

**What happened**
I should have known it was going to be a bad day when we all had to go to the hall for CDT. Guess what? I'm not doing design and technology until after Christmas because I'm a W for Wibberley which is nearly bottom of the alphabet. I have to do Food Technology with Mrs Kidner instead. No offence to Mrs Kidner—she seems OK—but I don't want to bake, I want to saw. As you can guess, I was a bit fed up at break, even after Clifford shoved some Year Eights out of the way and bought Chloe and me a flapjack. He wouldn't let us pay. He's kind, if a bit weird. The flapjack was just right—not too hard or too sweet but Chloe threw hers in the bin as soon as Clifford turned his back. It was then the trouble started. I asked her why she'd thrown hers

away and she said she wasn't eating anything *he'd* touched and I said that was mean and she said it was all right for me because I was immune to germs from hanging out with Melanie McCleod. I didn't say anything because there's no point with Chloe. What got me was that Josephine and Tamla laughed and they didn't even know Melanie.

Chloe made us sit behind Josephine and Tamla in English and kept whispering to them. Mr Pikelet kept giving us a look and I was worried we'd get a warning (two warnings = detention). He asked us to read out our words and he said mine were very well chosen but he just said 'OK' to Chloe's. She had only thought of three for each column, though, which can't have taken her the recommended twenty minutes, even if she'd done best handwriting. She scribbled 'swot' in pencil on the edge of my sheet. It's a good job I had my rubber.

Chloe was well behaved in history. Silence means silence with Mr Skibereen, you can just tell from the first second, but he wasn't as frightening as I thought he would be and he made the lesson interesting. He gave me a stamp for knowing what 'chronology' meant. Chloe sort of 'huhhed' under her breath but you can't just sit there and not say anything when you know the answer, can you?

I knew something was really wrong when she just went off with Josephine and Tamla at lunchtime without waiting for me to finish my spring roll. Then she didn't sit with me in Geography which was another sign. Last period was library time and she slid this note across to me during the explanation about the Dewey Decimal System.

> **Don't bother sitting with us anymore. We don't hang out with creeps or freaks.**

I began to shake when I read it but tried not to show I cared. When I got in I just went straight to my room. My mum's quite good at knowing when I'm ready to talk and when I'm not ready so she left me alone until after *EastEnders*. By then I'd got a bit wheezy because my asthma always sets off when I'm stressed but I still didn't tell her about the note. She wasn't going to let me go to school today but I didn't want to fall behind or be mollycoddled so I just let her write a little note about inhalers to Mr Curbishley in my planner in case.

I was OK when I set off first thing this morning because I thought Chloe and me might have a fresh start. Nearly every day in juniors Chloe would fall out one minute then say 'friends again?' the next but Chloe didn't sit with me in any lessons today or hang out with me at lunchtime so I went to Computer Club with Peter and Clifford instead. (The man in the orange shirt was there. His name is Mr Kanchelsis but everyone calls him Dave. He is in charge of special needs and tells jokes all the time. He told one about a man with a meat pie on his head but I wasn't in a laughing mood).

Chloe didn't speak until we were getting changed for PE last lesson and I discovered that I had sewn the tops of my socks together when I was putting the name tag in. Tamla laughed and Chloe and Josephine joined in. Tamla's laugh wasn't a nasty one, it was just normal because I suppose it did look funny but Chloe and Josephine's laugh was nasty. I tried to concentrate on putting my foot into my sock and ignoring them. Then Josephine said something like, 'How did you put up with that airhead so long?' and Chloe said, 'Don't ask me.'

I went red and my eyes prickled but I didn't say a thing. I just did PE without socks and Mrs Gallon, the PE teacher, didn't notice at all.

When I came home, Mum had found the note Chloe had written so I blurted everything out and had a proper cry—the one where you need tissues and your face goes salty and feels as if it's cracking. Mum was fuming and wanted to phone Mrs Shepherd and tell her what a spoilt brat of a daughter she had but Jem told her it was a waste of time because Mrs Shepherd was a snobby old bag and neither she nor Chloe were worth the hassle.

Before I went to bed, Mum came to my room and stroked my hair. She said maybe it was time to make some new friends if my old ones didn't deserve me and I suppose she's right. I just wasn't expecting to have to do it in the first week.

I can't write any more because we have to pick Mel up on the way to the rehearsal. At least I've got one friend left. Two, if you count Peter. Three, if you count Clifford. And I am doing well in school. I had a double stamp for that maths homework I told you about. Ten stamps in any subject means you get a certificate. Here's the maths for you to see. Excuse the bottom bit which got a bit blurry from my tears.

**Person 1: C Wibberley (my mum)**

Well! Well! Well!

A person goes to a well with two jars, one of which holds 3 pints and the other 5 pints. How can we bring back exactly 4 pints?

Presuming there is space in the jar holding three pints (see drawing) I would pour water from the jar with 5 pints into the jar with three pints until they are level. (see drawing)

The problem would be if the jars were not the same size because it doesn't say what size the jars are.
But 3 pints plus five pints = eight pints so equalled out it would be 4 pints plus 4 pints = eight pints.

Answer = 4?
(I'm sorry but it's a long time since I've done maths.)

**Person 2: D Wibberley (my dad)**

Drink 4 of them.

**Was there any difference in the ways the two people investigated the problem?**

Yes, my mum had to get all the jars out and measuring jugs in the kitchen and wrote everything down. It took her ages because she is very practical. My dad just did it in his head mentally without any jars because he is very mental. It's no use giving him questions about pints.

**Was one method more efficient than the other?**

I'm not sure. My mum's way took a long time but she set out all the steps. Dad's way was quicker but it is hard to know if he is right or not because he didn't show his working out.

**What does this tell you about maths?**

I'm going to fail.

Teacher's comment.

**No you are not going to fail, Simone!
You show good insight into mathematical thinking.
Keep it up!**

YOU'RE A STAR!

YOU'RE A STAR!

# Tonsils

(in case you get it mixed up with your appendix—ha!)


SUNDAY, SEPTEMBER 12TH

Dear Mr Cohen,

I know this is the end of Diary 1. I'm really looking forward to
Diary 2. One thing I need to ask is this—I'm not sure if you
want me to do Monday as well because I haven't done a
Monday yet because we started on a Tuesday. Mum says I've
written enough to keep you occupied until doomsday so not to
bother. If you do want Mondays, let me know and I'll post it
later.

   Don't forget either that if you want to see *Wind in the Willows*
it starts soon. I highly recommend it. You could bring your
girlfriend, if you've got one. There's a nice girl in Mayhem
Theatre Company called Vinora going free if you haven't.
Yours conscientiously,

Simone


PS Here's that page from my planner I told you about.
PPS I've had a big think this weekend and if Chloe wants to
hang out with people she's only known for a few days instead of
all her life, that's her decision. I've also decided that because we
go back a long way, I'll be available if she changes her mind, so
long as she doesn't send any more notes. Mum's made me
promise to show her any further notes instantly because notes
overstep the mark and I agree.

# September

**Attendance**

|  | Mon | Tue | Wed | Thu | Fri | Full Attendance | P = Present |
|---|---|---|---|---|---|---|---|
| am |  |  |  |  |  | ✓ | A = Absent |
| pm |  |  |  |  |  |  | L = Late |

## Mon 6

INSET

| | Homework | |
|---|---|---|
| | Date due | Done |
| | | |

## Tue 7

| | Homework | |
|---|---|---|
| | Date due | Done |
| Maths - Well, Well, Well investigation | Friday | ✓ |
| French - back book | Wed | ✓ |

## Wed 8

| | Homework | |
|---|---|---|
| | Date due | Done |
| Geography - finish map of the world | Thurs | ✓ |
| English - happy and sad word list | Thurs | ✓ |

48

# September

| Thur 9 | | Homework | |
|---|---|---|---|
| | | Date due | Done |
| | bring apron for food technology next week | 16 Sept | |
| | History - finish list of key words and definitions | Frid | ✓ |

| Fri 10 | | Homework | |
|---|---|---|---|
| | | Date due | Done |
| | Maths - finish p15 | Mond | |
| | English - read reading book and keep log | Frid | |

| Weekend | Weekend 11/12 |
|---|---|
| I wrote in my journal for Mr. Cohen's MA. | |

| Group Tutor | C Cumbrish ley |
|---|---|
| Parent/Guardian | C Webberley |
| Student | S. A. Wibberley |

Comments Please allow Simone to use her inhaler if she needs it — she has been feeling wheezy recently.

**Bartock University:**
Educational Studies Department

**Memo**

September 20th.

Dear Simone,

I guess I shouldn't enter into correspondence with my research subjects but I'm making an exception in your case. I just wanted to say thank you for the incredible detail of your journal—it's very helpful. My tutor, Professor Shingle is <u>so</u> impressed—and that's no easy feat! The professor could take on Mrs Bent in a misery guts competition and win hands down any day but don't tell either of them I said so!

Don't worry about the Monday—I have plenty of data to process from your first four days, thank you.

Incidentally, Mr English is a friend of mine—we trained together and I know he's finding it difficult to cope with everything at Bartock High, so just keep an eye on him for me. Thanks for the invitation to *Wind in the Willows*. I don't have a girlfriend to bring but I do have a partner—Gareth— and we'll try to get along to the show one evening.

The next form from me will be just before Christmas.

Best wishes,

*Ben*

Ben Cohen

# Questionnaire 2:

**To be completed at the <u>end</u> of the Autumn Term.**

**Name:**

Simone Wibberley

# Questionnaire

Please answer as fully as possible. Thank you
**Date:** December 19th

**These questions relate back to your first questionnaire.**

## Section 1

In questionnaire 1 you listed the following as things you were <u>most</u>
looking forward to at Bartock High:
1. **Being treated like a grown up**
2. **Facilities and trips**
3. **Wider choice of teachers**
4. **School meals**
5. **CDT**

**Have these things changed during your first term?**

I will try to be detailed in my replies, Mr Cohen, because I know it's
important but it is nearly Christmas and an awkward time to be filling in
forms, no offence. I haven't even wrapped half my presents yet, plus I've got
to work out what to buy for Clifford because he bought me something and I
didn't get him anything. I know if you are given a gift at Christmas it doesn't
mean you have to give one back and I already get teased enough about
Clifford being my boyfriend (which he is not—no way) but he bought lots of
people presents and nobody gave him one back and that's unseasonal. I don't
even know his postcode.

52

# The Answers

## 1. Being treated like a grown up

Some teachers treat you like a grown up but others don't. So I suppose that's a yes/no answer. That's all I have to say on this subject, for now.

## 2. The trips

Trips at Bartock are miles better because they aren't linked to topics all the time. Like in Year Six the only trip we went on was to the Dream-ee Toffee factory when Anthony Bent pushed me in some icing sugar and gave me the worst asthma attack I'd ever had. We did go to see *Oliver!* at the theatre after but that was only so Mrs Bent could prevent a law suit. At Bartock High I've been on two trips to the bowling alley with a McDonald's after and last week was the Year Seven to Nine's disco, not to mention non-uniform days. There's a French trip at Easter but I don't know if I can go yet because of the money. In July there's something called an activities week when you don't have any lessons and everyone just does whatever they want, even the teachers. I can't imagine Mrs Bent ever letting that happen in a zillion years.

## Facilities

Facilities are miles better. Here's a comparison chart which you might find useful.

| Facility | Woodhill Road | Bartock High |
|---|---|---|
| Sports facilities | Dining Room<br>1 Football pitch (sloping)<br>Playground | 1 huge Sports Hall<br>4 Netball/tennis courts<br>3 Football and rugby and hockey pitches |
| Art and Craft | Paint table near the sink for one group at a time when Mrs Hunt comes in on a Wednesday<br>1 cupboard | 2 Food and technology rooms with cookers and fridges and microwaves<br>2 Design rooms with workbenches and goggles and jigsaws<br>2 Art rooms with charcoal and plastics and mod-rok and everything the artist needs |
| IT | 8 computers in the resources area that you can only use on a rota if the teacher remembers | 2 suites of computers and scanners and Internets and the latest technology newspaper coupons can buy |
| Library | Behind the computers in the resources area | A special room with carousels full of books and nice tables and quiet areas where you can go if you want a bit of peace at lunchtimes away from people bugging you |
| Extras | Lost property box<br>Wildlife garden (out of bounds) | 2 drinks machines<br>a part-time nurse in a proper sick bay<br>minibus (though it's falling to bits) |
| Personal belongings | Own peg in cloakroom | Lockers but they are miles away in your form room and you can't go in if there's a lesson so they're not much use and you end up carting all your stuff around with you anyway |

So, to summarize therefore, facilities are better at secondary except for the locker business but I suppose you wouldn't expect a primary school to have a sports hall and science labs and art rooms and lockers and drinks machines so although it's a yes, it's a bit of an unfair yes.

## 3. Wider Choice of teachers

This is a definite yes.

## 4. School Meals

Another most definite yes.

## 5. CDT

It will be a yes when I do it after Christmas.

So that's 3 yeses, a yes/no, and one no, Mr Cohen, for your bar chart or database of your choice.

# Section 2

You were not looking forward to:
1. **Getting lost on the first day**
2. **Losing bus pass/wrong bus**
3. **Possibility of bullies**
4. **Detention for falling behind, especially in maths**
5. **Friendships not working out**
6. **Asthma attacks during school**

**Did any of these things happen?**

## The Answers

### Getting lost
I did not get lost on the first day or after that. We had a map of the school in our planners. Sometimes the Year Eights told us to get lost but that's Year Eights for you.
To summarize therefore: It is no longer a worry or a problem.

### Losing my bus pass
I have not lost my bus pass at all because I always keep it in the same place so I know exactly where it is. Peter has lost his loads of times but his photograph is now legendary and he keeps having it returned.
To summarize therefore: It is no longer one of my worries or problems.

### Naughty Kids in Class/Bullying
There have been some problems with bullying at school but no stabbings like Anthony teased me about in the hairdressers that time. The good thing about when someone is bullied is the teachers sort it out quickly with no messing and we talk about it in Form Time and PSE. I haven't been properly bullied. I've already told you that some of the Year Eights shove us about in

the dinner queue and say things like 'move out of the way, you little ****s' but it's not personal and you get used to it.

I have suffered from the silent treatment and daggers. (see under friendships)

## Naughty Kids

There are naughty kids in my class but there are always naughty kids in every class. In 7DC we have four but it could be worse. 7AW has five and the whole of 7HR has a bad reputation. Mrs Warrener is always making them stand up in assembly and show the rest of the school what a rabble they are.

The naughty kids in my class are, in order of naughtiness:

| | |
|---|---|
| Clifford Hammond | (17 detentions so far) |
| Chloe M. Shepherd | (6 detentions so far) |
| Josephine Lyons | (6 detentions so far) |
| Peter Bacon | (3 detentions so far) |

Melanie was right about Clifford Hammond—he won't do anything he is told, even for Mr Kanchelsis. He's had tonnes of detentions, which is a miracle for someone who doesn't ever speak. The only person he communicates with is Peter. Mr Kanchelsis told me Clifford is an elective mute, which means he could talk if he felt like it but he doesn't feel like it. Melanie told me Clifford used to speak but he got so ticked off with his mum and dad always telling him to shut up, he did.

The embarrassing thing is Clifford still buys me a flapjack every break. I don't know whether it's embarrassing because he is the naughtiest kid in our class or embarrassing because I'm fed up with flapjacks and wouldn't mind an iced bun or just an apple instead. Peter is mainly told off for forgetting his homework and not listening and drawing hand grenades on the teachers' worksheets but the other three are properly naughty. Chloe and Josephine are so bad they could fit into Year Eight tomorrow, no problem. They go everywhere together, even the toilet. In lessons they whisper all the time and giggle and point to certain boys and send them love notes. In other words, they act like boring girlie-girls which is annoying to other girls who want to be taken seriously and use hegner-saws or become accountants in multi-national companies.

And they never listen. I'm sorry to report their behaviour is especially awful in French. Unfortunately, Mr English doesn't have very good control and sometimes I think he is going to cry. I have tried to make them be quiet for him but then they give me daggers and Chloe's daggers can really hurt, unless you're immune.

To summarize therefore, I was right to worry about naughty kids but I don't need to worry too much as long as it doesn't get personal. It's alarming to think that 2 out of 4 of the worst kids in my class are from Woodhill Primary. Mrs Bent would be appalled if she knew. She might not be surprised at Peter but she would at Chloe.

### Falling behind, especially in maths

I haven't fallen behind. I do my homework straight away and keep up with everything. I'm doing fine in maths. I think it's because Mrs Ruskin explains things properly and doesn't make you feel small if you get things wrong or say to the whole class: 'Here we go again, Simone. Who else hasn't been listening and needs to wash their ears out?' like Mrs Bent used to. To prove I haven't fallen behind, here's a copy of my mid-year assessment sheet we got in November. Dad was so proud he gave me five pounds but that could have been guilt because he forgot to turn up for the parents' consultation evening.

# Name: Simone Wibberley Form: 7DC

| Subject | Effort | Behaviour | Comments |
|---|---|---|---|
| Art | 1 | A | Simone has made a good start |
| Drama | 1 | A | Enthusiastic and confident. |
| English | 1 | A | Excellent – a star! |
| French | 1 | A | One of the more pleasant members of the form |
| Geography | 1 | A | A sound start. |
| History | 1 | A | A most polite pupil. |
| Maths | 1 | A | Always tries |
| Science | 1 | A | Good all round |
| IT | 1 | A | Shows good understanding. |
| Technology | 2 | A | Simone tries hard after a shaky start |
| PSE | 2 | A | A little quiet at times |
| Games | 1 | A | Growing in self confidence. |
| Music | 2 | B | Might benefit from changing groups |

**Codes for effort:**

1 = excellent    2 = above average    3 = average

4 = below average    5 = basic level

Codes for behaviour:

A B C    excellent/acceptable/needs improvement

Attendance: 95%

Punctuality: Excellent

Standard of Uniform: Excellent

Signature of tutor: C Cumbershley

Signature of Head of Year: P. Wawrener

To summarize, therefore, I have not fallen behind, though if you asked Chloe she would be forced to say she had definitely fallen behind. Mr and Mrs Shepherd were called in to school to see Mr Curbishley because her report was in the 'needs improvement' category all the way through. Mr Curbishley may be a maverick, but he's an observant maverick who doesn't let things slip. In a strange way, he's a lot like Mrs Bent for strictness, except he doesn't wear Hush Puppies.

I found out that Chloe really got it in the neck when she went home because Mr Shepherd suffers from workaholicism and hardly ever leaves his shop in daylight. They grounded her for two weeks but she only did one night of it because she warned them she'd phone Childline and the police would arrest them like that case in the paper and who would operate the steam machine then?

I bet you think it's a shame Chloe wanted to go through puberty instead of helping you with your experiment, Mr Cohen. She would have made a good subject, wouldn't she?

## Detentions

I have had one detention, from Mrs Kidner the food technology teacher but Mum sorted it and I didn't have to do it. It was a while ago now but I have kept photocopied documentation for you as I thought it might help your research. Dad didn't mention photocopying cost this time because he's the main reason I got a detention anyway so he couldn't refuse.

It all started when I was staying at my dad's and needed ingredients for Lemon Crunch Pie. These were the ingredients:

100g (4oz) digestive biscuits
50g (2oz) margarine or butter
1 small can of evaporated milk
1/2 a pack jelly
fresh fruit to decorate

Dad didn't have one thing from my list, not even margarine. He always says he is too tired to cook and why bother when Colonel Sanders lives next door? He said I could take in a packet of Jelly Tots for the jelly but I didn't think it would work because the colours would all squidge into one giant mess. Trouble was, he didn't have any of the ingredients for the week before with the Fish and Tomato Casserole or the week before that with the Quick Bread Buns, and Mrs Kidner's patience finally ran out.

Mrs Kidner wrote this in my planner.

**Comments**                    **October 14th**

**Notice of detention: Simone will have to attend lunchtime detention tomorrow as a sanction for forgetting her ingredients for food technology three weeks in a row.**

JKidner

This was my Mum's reply:

October 15th

Dear Mrs Kidner,
Regarding Simone's detention for forgetting her
ingredients.
I refuse permission for Simone to attend this
detention. Simone does not deliberately forget
her ingredients but as she stays at her father's
house on a Wednesday night and as his idea of
fresh food is curry sauce and chips from The
Frying Pan, she does not have access to such
things as self-raising flour or fresh eggs or fresh
anything. Should you like to give *him* a detention,
his number is on her contact form.

C Webberley.

This was Mrs Kidner's reply to my mum's reply:

Dear Mrs Wibberley,                    October 15th

Thank you for your note about Simone. Had I realized her
circumstances I would not have set the detention. The
problem of her lack of ingredients for lessons still
remains, however. Perhaps she could bring them in on
Wednesday mornings and leave them with me until her
lesson on Thursday?

J Kidner

Then my dad saw what Mum and Mrs Kidner had written in my planner so he replied:

> Dear Mrs Kidner,
> There's no need for Simone to bring anything in early for cookery. She'll have everything she needs, freshly grown by Greenpeace from now on.
>
> Yours,
> Dennis Wibberley
>
> The News Shack (open from 7.00am–7.00pm except Sundays i.e. 12 hours a day with not much time off for buying pineapple chunks or faffing about in theatres)

There were also a lot of phone calls between Mum and Dad that went with these letters but I wasn't allowed to tape them for you, mainly because of the bad language. I felt horrible because Mum said I should have told her sooner about the ingredients seeing as I knew as well as anybody what a waste of space Dennis was, but if I had told her she might have stopped my Wednesday experiment and I like sleeping over at Dad's. Dad went totally over the top with all the recipes for the rest of the term and that made me feel worse because once he had to go to the supermarket for dried yeast and he's allergic to places that are out to crush the independent retailer.

Mrs Kidner always smiles at me now and asks me if I'm all right and pats me on the shoulder. I'll be glad when I swap over after Christmas and I can get down to CDT, a subject which is kinder to children with two homes and doesn't involve ingredients and threats of court actions for libel.

To summarize, therefore I have not had a detention (not one that was my fault, anyway).

## Friendships not working out

I was right about this one, wasn't I? Maybe I'm psychic.

Like I said earlier, Chloe hangs out with Josephine Lyons all the time now, though we are back on speaking terms. Things were worse straight after the note in the library (see Diary 1). They never said anything directly horrible to me but they did things like ignore me in the corridor and walked the other way if I came towards them (also known as the silent treatment). I pretended I didn't care and just got on with my work and spent lunchtimes at Computer Club or in the library. I was a bit lonely in lessons, especially when you had to work in pairs, like music or PRSE, because I always ended up in a three with Clifford and Peter which isn't much fun when you have to discuss something and one of your group is drawing automatic weapons and the other doesn't do discussion. Mum wrote to Mr Curbishley about it in my planner even though I asked her not to:

Mr Curbishley –

I am concerned that Simone does not seem to be making many new friends. Could you ask her teachers how she is getting on in lessons, please?

*C Webberley.*

Simone always seems bright and cheerful but I will ask around. We have a parents' evening coming up where we can discuss your concerns further.

*C Curbishley*

Luckily I was all right by then because the week before parents evening Tamla had a massive row with Chloe and Josephine in the dinner queue and threw Sunny Delight over Chloe's sweatshirt. Mrs Shepherd came storming in to school the next day and Mrs Warrener had to calm her down in the hospitality suite.

I'm not sure what happened after that but during science Tamla asked if she could hang-out with me because Josephine was turning into the biggest pain in the butt ever and Chloe already was the biggest pain in the butt ever.

I didn't say 'yes' until two days later because I didn't want to be a rebound girlfriend. Alexis got a rebound boyfriend called Jake after breaking up with my dad and he turned out to be unsavoury. They've finished now, but only after Jake stole all her credit cards, even the one for Miss Selfridge. Alexis was so upset she turned to drink for comfort and met my dad in The Thirsty Farmer. They got back together again so I suppose she's dad's ex-ex-girlfriend now. He still uses his computer a lot, though, and Alexis is retaining her independence by keeping her exercise bike and ceramic frog collection at her mum's house for the time being.

Tamla has sort of grown on me. We sit together in class and she phones me at night to ask about homework, usually because she can't read what she's written down in her planner. She tries to do shorthand like her journalist ancestors but really it's just a mass of squiggles that no one can read. I like Tamla but I can't talk about juniors with her and say things like 'Do you remember that time Anthony Bent wet his pants on the swimming bus?' as I could with Chloe. Tamla understands though and says she feels the same about her and Josephine. Chloe sent me a Christmas card, though, and I sent her one but we didn't exchange gifts. It's the first Christmas I haven't bought her anything since we were five. She bought Josephine a *Now that's what I call music 59* CD and some eye shadow. I don't wear make-up so the gift would have been wasted on me, anyway.

I asked Jem if having a bad friend like Chloe was worse than having no friends at all. He said in his opinion it was worse, but that friendship is the hardest nut to crack, though it got easier as you got older. Jem is so wise. No wonder he became an actor.

One other hard thing has been with Melanie. I've tried to keep it the same but she thinks I'm being funny because I can't go to her house as much as I used to at juniors. She doesn't understand about homework and dark nights. It's going to be great this holiday, though, because her Uncle LeeRoy is being released on parole in time for Christmas and he can do really good tricks with his six-pack and an empty coke can.

### 7. Asthma Attacks in School

So far I haven't had an attack at school but we have an excellent nurse on the premises called Mrs Ellis who can deal with anything. The only time I feel a bit wheezy is during Games but Mrs Gallon lets me sit out immediately. I think I might be growing out of asthma now, anyway. I get greasy hair instead and have to use Pantene.

### Primary School
### Is there anything you still miss about Woodhill Primary School?

Not really because I still see Melanie and I've grown out of everything else. I saw Mrs Arundel (Miss Cassidy) in Dad's shop last week and she sent her regards to you.


# Section 3

### Have any new problems emerged that you didn't have before?

Not really, because Chloe has been my only problem and I had her before. There's a rumour going round that we're having our TB jabs the day we get back from the Christmas holidays. Luther, Peter's brother, told us the jab kills because it has six needles and each needle is ten centimetres long. This is quite worrying for someone like me who has thin arms.

### Thank you for completing the second questionnaire. The next diary will be sent to you shortly after the New Year.
### B. Cohen

You're welcome, Mr Cohen. I wrote tonnes more than I thought I would. Not enough to need spiral binding though, like I suppose Anthony's will. Joyeux Noel.

MERRY CHRISTMAS

I did this for you on Dad's computer. You don't have to put it in your survey. I've asked for clothes vouchers for Christmas and a Black and Decker workmate. What have you asked for?

To
Mr Cohen and Gareth
have a brilliant
Christmas
and a
Happy New Year
Best Wishes from
Simone

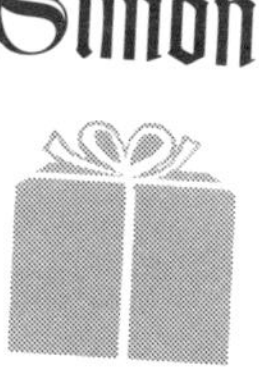

Chard Halls,
**Bartock University Campus**
Bartock

Jan 4th

Dear Simone,

Find enclosed a diary for you to complete as near to the
beginning of term as possible. This will allow me to compare
the start of your first term with that of your second term.
Have a Happy New Year.
Best wishes

Ben

Ben Cohen

PS Thank you for the Christmas card, Simone.
Although Gareth and I don't actually celebrate
Christmas because we are Jewish, it was a
kind gesture on your part.

**Bartock University:**
Department of Education

# Pupil's Diary

To be completed at the beginning of the Spring Term

**Name: Simone Wibberley**

**Just a note before I start**

I didn't know you were Jewish, Mr Cohen. Jewish children are lucky because they can have a relaxing time over ~~Chris~~ the festive season without their parents arguing about whose turn it is to have them on Christmas Day this year and whose turn it is to have them on Boxing Day instead, though if I were Jewish I'd miss having presents and decorating the tree. Don't you get any presents at all? Not even socks?

Yours sincerely

Simone


PS You'll probably find this diary shorter than the last one because Mum thinks I give too much of our personal lives away and I have to concentrate on the bits between catching the bus at 8.10a.m. and getting off the bus at 4.25p.m., though she agreed I could include homework (5.30–6.30–7.00p.m.) and if people from school call or sleep over. Subjects that she says are not going to help you gain an MA are:

1. Details of arguments between her and Dad.
2. The state of the Wibberley's finances (either household).
3. Dad's drinking habits, deplorable though they are.
4. Her opinions of Alexis, valid as they are.
5. Dad's opinions of Jem, unreasonable as they are.

I don't know why she's so fussy all of a sudden but if it's any consolation, Dad said he isn't bothered what I write about him as long as I mention what a fantastic father he is. He also says to tell you he's got some *Viz* Annuals left over if you're interested. They're half price.

## FRIDAY 7TH JANUARY

Did not want to get up this morning because it was freezing and it seems unfair starting back on a Friday. I nearly missed the bus but luckily Hazel was late, too. I asked her if she'd had a nice holiday and she said it was all right except her husband had slipped his disc on New Year's Eve dancing to hits from the Eighties. I thought that was a bit strange because the music was slow in olden times but I didn't say anything.

Luther went on about TB jabs again but my mum had explained about the six needles only being a tester and nowhere near ten centimetres long, so I just told Luther to buzz off, which he did, but only after pulling Peter's tie so tight he nearly strangled his own brother. Luther makes me glad I'm an only child.

Clifford was waiting for Peter and me as we disembarked. I like the word disembarked — it's written on the bus and means 'to get off' and doesn't have anything to do with dogs or trees. Anyway, Clifford was holding his copy of *The Rotten Romans* that I had sent him and grinning as if it was still Christmas, then he gave me this tiny envelope with this even tinier note inside.

I didn't know what to say, because Melanie's my best friend, but I didn't want to hurt his feelings, either, so I just said thanks. I feel sorry for Clifford because Melanie told me the council are going to evict the Hammonds for anti-social behaviour as soon as the court order comes through. Mrs McCleod said it's a shame for the kids because they'll probably end up in care.

Mr Cohen, you know last time you asked about anything I missed about primary school and I said no, only Melanie? I've thought of another one. I miss being able to sidle in at lunchtimes to talk to Miss Cassidy. She was always putting up displays so you could ask if she needed help and she always said yes and while you passed her a picture or the staple gun you could casually mention what was worrying you and she would listen and nod and advise.

In secondary school, you aren't allowed in at lunchtimes and even when you are nobody puts up displays unless it's an art room, not even the mavericks. If you have a problem you can go to the staff room and ask to see the member of staff of your choice but you can't *sidle*. If we could sidle, I'd ask how you can tell somebody who might need help but doesn't talk, that you are on their side but to call it a day on the cards and flapjacks, without causing psychological damage.

Anyway, that was just a thought. I don't know whether you'll have to add it to your new bar chart or put it in an old one.

School was OK. Tamla was away today and Josephine had music practice during PE so I worked in a pair with Chloe on feinting and dodging skills. It felt funny being a partner with Chloe again, but almost normal too. Mrs Gallon was pleased with the activity we made up and we had to show it to the rest of the class. I dodged and Chloe feinted, then we swapped round. Mrs Gallon gave us a merit mark each. Chloe was really chuffed because she doesn't get many merit marks now that her behaviour leaves much to be desired.

After school I did my homework. Jem is away until the end of the week because he's being Aladdin Mucky Tights in Blandford Forum, so it was just Mum and me. Mum was doing her college homework, too, so we didn't chat much, except to say pass the skint coffee biscuits (Rich Tea, get it?). Just before I went to bed, Mrs Shepherd phoned and asked to speak to me and said how delighted she was that Chloe had been given a merit mark in PE, especially as the school seems to have it in for her, and would I like to come round after school one day next week? It's the first time I've been invited round to Chloe's for centuries. I said I'd think about it because it depended on my other commitments, such as taking regular showers and homework. Mrs Shepherd said that was odd because Chloe hardly ever had any homework and I said, 'That is odd because I have heaps and we're in the same class.' She said, 'I see' and hung up.

**Important Point:** There's tonnes and tonnes more homework at secondary school than at primary school, Mr Cohen. I didn't put that in the other questionnaire, either, because I've only just thought of it but it's fact, not opinion. Mr Skibereen has been teaching us the difference. I can provide evidence, if you need it. All I have to do is photocopy any week from my planner, or let you feel the weight of my school bag. My mum weighed my school bag once — it came to over 14lbs (5kg to you and me). Mum's going to bring it up at parents' evening and might do an essay on it for her physiotherapy course.

## SATURDAY 8TH JANUARY
Not vital for your MA (no offence)

## SUNDAY 9TH JANUARY
Not vital for your MA (no offence)

## MONDAY 10TH JANUARY

I had a shock today, though you probably already knew about it, Mr Cohen. Anthony Bent has left Alabaster Boys and has become a pupil at Bartock High School. Worse, he's with me in 7DC. I couldn't believe it when Mr Curbishley introduced us to a new member of the form during registration and Benty was standing there. Benty told us at  break that he'd left Alabaster's because the travelling was proving to be rather more of an obstacle than anticipated. Chloe said that was a load of porkies because her dad had heard that Anthony was being bullied and that his mother thought it was best to move him back to being with his friends, despite the consequences as far as university was concerned. I feel sorry for Anthony if he was being bullied but I can't help remembering the conversation about blood and bandages in the hairdressers that time. To use one of Mr Pikelet's favourite words, it seems ironical. And I don't know why he's been put with us because he never hung around with us at Woodhill. He always said we were lesser mortals than him.

Apart from that, school was fine. In PE today we had to continue with the dodging and practise our feinting in fours. Chloe and I showed Tamla and Josephine what to do and we made up a great game called Dodge Death. Tamla thought of the title and I thought of the rules. I think it could catch on, because it's more dangerous than netball and you don't need to be tall like in basketball. Near the end, I became a bit wheezy and Chloe said, 'Shall I fetch your inhaler?' like she used to.

Last of all was science with Mr Curbishley. We started a new topic called Growing Up which will include details of sexual reproduction and he hopes we'll all impress him by being sensible about it. He gave us a list of useful words to learn. Some are easy like 'egg' and 'baby' but I had to help Peter with the longer ones like 'fertilization' and 'placenta'. Anthony, who was sitting in front, turned round and said: 'Don't tell me you still can't read, Streaky,' and snorted in that snobby way he has. Clifford heard and gave him a dead-eye. Clifford's dead-eyes are even worse than Chloe's because he usually follows them up with an ankle crop, so Anthony had better watch it or he'll be back to square one on the bullying.

About five seconds after I arrived home, Mrs Shepherd phoned and asked to speak to me again. She wanted to know if we'd been given any homework and I said yes, just science. There was a pause, then she asked what so I told her we had to familiarize ourselves with the word list. There was another pause and I heard her say 'word list' and she said, 'Chloe seems to have mislaid hers,' and I said, 'Tell  her it's the one that starts with adolescence and ends with vagina.' There was a much longer pause, then Mrs Shepherd said I'd been very helpful and not to forget to pop round one day. For some reason my mum was cracked up on the floor laughing after I'd hung up. Mr Curbishley would not have been impressed.

TUESDAY JANUARY 11TH

Ozzy, Hazel's son, was driving the bus today because Hazel had to go with her husband to check his back out. Ozzy's real job is as a DJ at Lazer Rave's in town. I think he'd come straight from work because he still had bits of silly string in his hair. Either that or he's got a major dandruff problem. All the Year Nine and Ten girls stood round the front to talk to him because they think he's fit. That doesn't mean he goes to a gym, Mr Cohen, in case you were wondering, it means he's handsome. It's a good job Chloe doesn't come to school by bus because she'd never disembark.

Speaking of Chloe, she was acting weird today. She kept putting her hand up in lessons and answering questions. I wasn't surprised in science because she started puberty early and reads *J17* so you could say Growing Up is her specialist topic but she doesn't usually bother for English or maths. Anthony looked a bit miffed because he doesn't like competition. On the way to French, Chloe told Tamla and me that her parents had turned cool and were paying her to do her schoolwork. She will get ten pounds for every merit mark and an extra twenty for a headteacher's award. If Mum or Dad or Jem gave me ten pounds for every merit I'd had, I would have three hundred and fifty pounds by now but I just know my mum would have three hundred and fifty fits if I even mentioned being paid.

In French, Mr English looked scared at first when Chloe put her hand up because she usually only does it to be rude but after a while he realized she was being serious and gave her two merit marks — her first twenty pounds — just for saying: '*Non, merci, c'est tout,*' which anyone else would only have got one merit mark for, or even a half.

After school Melanie phoned to ask me to lend her my Tudors project from last year because Mrs Bent said they had to do some research and she couldn't go to the library because her mum had sold her last lot of library books in a car boot sale by accident. Before Mel hung up she told me that the police had been outside the Hammonds' house all day but she didn't know any details because McCleods automatically draw the curtains when they see blue flashing lights.

After that I packed my things for staying over at Dad's tomorrow and wrote this.


WEDNESDAY 12TH JANUARY

Chloe and Josephine asked Tamla and me if we wanted to go to Taunton on the train with them on Saturday. Taunton's nearly twenty miles away and massive compared to Bartock. I haven't been on my own before but I feel ready for the experience. Tamla said she might have her ears pierced again, seeing as the hole in her nose has almost healed with lack of use and Mrs Warrener wasn't going to relax the rules on body piercing.

At break, Clifford gave me the flapjack then darted away. It's his tradition. Chloe laughed and said, 'He's got the hots for you, Simone,' and I said, 'We're just friends', and Josephine said, 'Yeah, and we all know what kind of friends.' I didn't like being teased so I threw the flapjack away to show them I wasn't in love with Clifford or anything like that.

The rest of my day was normal. I've settled in to everything now, Mr Cohen, so I don't have that much to say about school, really, unless something unusual happens and nothing did.

After school I walked to The News Shack. Dad was still serving and Alexis was sleeping over at Toni's because Toni's life is going nowhere and she needs a friend right now, so I just went up to the flat and helped myself to a sandwich and did my homework until Dad finished. I noticed Alexis still hasn't moved her exercise bike but I didn't say anything in case it's a touchy subject.

Dad was so relieved when I told him he didn't have to buy me any more ingredients for food technology because I'd be starting CDT tomorrow he sent for pizzas to be delivered to the door like they do in American TV programmes. Then Mum phoned to say hello and to check if I'd done my homework and got clean knickers for tomorrow and eaten properly and I said yes to everything. Mum's got worse about organizing since the episode with the Lemon Crunch Pie. She doesn't give my dad credit for anything and I can tell it annoys him and that makes me feel bad. I didn't say anything though because she agreed I could go to Taunton on Saturday if I made proper arrangements about buses and don't talk to anyone suspicious, and that means either with or without a balaclava.

Today started off brilliantly because it was my first lesson of CDT. My teacher is called Mr O'Connell. I don't think he's a maverick because he wears thick black glasses and has a beard but he is certainly an expert in his field. The first lesson was quite ordinary because he had to explain about safety but that's only to be expected. Mr O'Connell showed us the equipment we'll be using, including a brand new electric saw. It was so cool. Chloe said there was no way she was putting her fingers anywhere near but I can't wait. Homework was to design a safety poster. Next week we have to design a plastic mould for a chocolate, which isn't as easy as it sounds because the chocolate can get stuck in the mould if the angle's wrong, leading to mess and disaster. It will be quite a challenge.

As you can imagine, Mr Cohen, I was in a great mood at break and was actually looking forward to my flapjack because I'd missed breakfast but just as Clifford handed it over to me, Chloe opened her big mouth and said, 'Shall I chuck it in the bin for you today or do you want to do it yourself, as usual, Simone?' I could feel my cheeks burning and Clifford just looked so miserable as he walked away. Peter gave me a daggers special and said, 'I didn't know you were like that, Wibbs.'

Afterwards, Chloe made out she was only trying to do me a favour but it didn't feel like one. I didn't see Clifford for the rest of the day because he kicked a hole in one of the boys' toilet doors and had to go to the Time Out Room with Mr Kanchelsis.

I tried to explain about the flapjack business to Pete on the way home but he just shrugged and said, 'Tell Cliff not me.'

I kept seeing Clifford's sad face when I was trying to do my safety poster and I didn't want any tea. It was my favourite pasta and spinach bake so Jem knew immediately there was a problem and asked what was wrong so I told him everything and he said, 'Right, get your coat, we're going to see the poor guy.' I was a bit surprised but in the car Jem told me he'd once fallen out with his friend called Stan and Stan had been knocked down the next day and died. Jem's never liked to leave things unsaid or unsettled since because, like Stan, you never know what's round the corner, and I agree. We called in at Melanie's first for directions but Mrs McCleod told us the Hammonds had already gone and the council had boarded all the windows up to stop them getting back in. We stayed for a cup of tea and some Battenberg and Melanie asked about the Tudor stuff but I'd forgotten it.

Back home, Jem suggested that I should write Clifford a letter because it's sometimes easier to write feelings than to say them, but I had to remember to be honest in what I put. I finished my safety poster first then wrote to Clifford. You can have a copy of the letter for your file. I guess your friendship section must be getting pretty thick by now.

> Dear Clifford,
> I am sorry about what happened at break. The truth is I am a bit fed up with flapjacks (no offence) but I should have told you myself instead of Chloe doing it like that. I hope you'll still be my friend.
> Simone Anna Wibberley 7DC

I think I succeeded in keeping the letter short but inoffensive.

FRIDAY 14TH JANUARY

I couldn't give Clifford the note directly because he was still on report for kicking the door in so I handed it to Mr Kanchelsis to pass on to him. Chloe was showing off because some boy in 8HL had wolf whistled at her in the haunted corridor. She went on and on about it as if it was the most important thing in the world but you can't say anything to her or you get accused of being jealous, even when you're definitely not. At lunchtime Peter handed me this note from Cliff.

The Romans kept dormice in special jars and fattened them up with walnuts and acorns. When there was no space left and the jars cracked, the Romans knew it was time to eat the dormice. They stuffed them with pork sausage meat.
Your sincerely

*Clifford Hammond*

I showed the note to my mum because it seemed a strange reply but she thinks Clifford had copied out something he found interesting to share with me and it was a sign of forgiveness.

Chloe phoned tonight and was on for about an hour making arrangements about going to Taunton tomorrow and telling me which shops we *just had* to go in. About a second after she hung up, Melanie called round unexpectedly for the Tudor project. She seemed in a real mardy that I had to search for it and she wouldn't stay for a drink because her dad was waiting in the van. Mum noticed Mel's mood, too, and asked if we'd fallen out. I said no but I had to think about it and realized the last time we'd had a good laugh together could have been in Tudor times too. I discussed it with my mum and she said now that I was at secondary maybe I had outgrown Melanie without knowing it because it wasn't like me to be so indifferent to my friends' needs. Mum does nag when Dad is the subject but she's usually very good on friendships, so I started to have a deeper think, but Chloe distracted me with another call, saying she could lend me some of her clothes if I needed something trendy to wear round town so that I wouldn't feel the odd one out.

I thought she was being generous for a minute but because I was in a deep thinking mood I realized she'd just served up a Chloe Shepherd special—a favour that isn't really a favour at all, just like with Clifford yesterday and too many other times to mention. I phoned her back straightaway and told her I didn't want to borrow any of her clothes, thanks, because I wasn't going into Taunton. I didn't say why, I just left it. Then I phoned Tamla to cancel and she said she wasn't bothered about going that much, either, so we arranged to meet in Bartock instead. After that I went back to my think about Melanie. My conclusion was that I should have given her the Tudor project earlier because I know what Mrs Bent's like about deadlines and I am always doing homework when she phones but I don't think I've grown out of her. I phoned her up to say sorry and to ask her if she wanted to come to Bartock tomorrow with Tamla and me and she said she would. Tamla isn't the sort to want me all to herself like Chloe did so being in a three should work but I won't be able to let you know until next time.


## A Query

I've been having a think about your experiment, Mr Cohen, and I'm worried I might be doing it wrong for you. This diary seems to be more about friendships and arguments than lessons and learning. If I am doing it wrong, you will let me know, won't you? I'd hate you to not get your MA because of me. What you could do, if my answers are not exactly what you want, is let me have samples of other Year Sevens' replies. It always helps me in maths when Mrs Ruskin gives examples on the board. I would also know if I was normal. You don't have to give me names or anything like that, though I am good at keeping secrets. And you needn't put any of Anthony's answers in because I wouldn't have thought he was a typical Year Seven.

Thank you.

Simone

Chard Halls,
**Bartock University Campus**
Bartock

June 12th

Dear Simone,

Find enclosed the final questionnaire and the answer to your query. I'm sorry it's taken so long to reply but it got wedged between all my papers and I have only just found it! Obviously, I can't reveal details of the other children taking part but I can let you in on some of my early findings, then you can work out for yourself whether you are normal or not!

I started off with thirty-five Y6 pupils in the survey but two left the area early on and five dropped out after the first questionnaire. Of the 28 left:

100% felt they had been well prepared for secondary school.

95% settled in to Y7 in either less than a week or within a few weeks.

98% found the concerns they had (losing bus passes etc) were never realized.

98% found either homework or the size of the school the biggest change.

96% liked being at secondary school more than primary.

94% have kept old friends *and* made new ones.

Only three of the pupils I surveyed were still unsettled and finding friendships difficult (No, you were not one of them, before you ask. You seem to cope really well with your problems).

If these results reflect Y7 pupils throughout the country I think it gives a positive message for parents and Y6 pupils worrying about starting secondary school, don't you? I hope you feel reassured.

That leaves only the enclosed simple questionnaire for you to complete. I was going to ask everyone to fill in a final diary but a comment you made in Diary 2 about 'being settled now and not having much to say unless something unusual happens' led me to reassess the need for a third one and I decided against it. To be honest, only you and you-know-who have completed the survey in any real detail—I am lucky to have 'yes', 'no', and 'sometimes' from most of the participants and that's after a million reminders! Without getting too technical, my main field of research was always the transfer period between leaving primary and starting secondary anyway and I have all that information now. All this final questionnaire will do is 'round off' the evidence. What I have to do next is interview primary and secondary school teachers and heads of department, then collate all the information and hope Prof Shingle is happy. Wish me luck!

Thank you once again for taking part in my 'experiment', Simone. Your answers have always been so detailed and delightful, I feel I've really got to know you well. Give my best wishes to both your families and good luck in Year Eight.

Shalom!

Ben

# Questionnaire 3:

**Final term**

**Name:**

Simone Wibberley

(PUPIL COPY)

Shalom, Mr Cohen! (I use shalom loads. It's wicked having a word that means hello *and* goodbye. I wish I were doing Jewish instead of French because there wouldn't be as much vocab to learn. Mr English always gives us stacks, even

if his classroom management is smitten with errors. Here is your last questionnaire (boo hoo!) I've added bits because that's the kind of person I am.

Simone

**Bartock University:**
Department of Educational Studies
# Final Questionnaire

Please tick the boxes. One tick per section please.
**To be returned by:** July 7th

**1. How settled do you feel at school:**
Very settled ☑
Settled ☐
Fairly settled ☐
Not settled ☐

**2. Has life at secondary school been what you expected?**
Yes, it's better ☑
No, it's worse ☐
Don't know ☐

**3. Do you feel your standard of work has changed since you started Y7?**
Yes, it's better ☑
Yes, it's worse ☐
Same ☐
Don't know ☐

**4. Do you feel your friendships have changed since you started Y7?**
Yes, they're better ☑
Yes, they're worse ☐
Same ☐
Don't know ☐

This was a short one, Mr. Cohen!

**My added bits**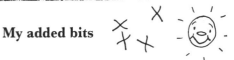

I can't believe I've nearly done a whole year at secondary school, Mr Cohen. It doesn't seem two minutes since Mum found your form in my old school bag and told me to either fill it in or throw it away. I'm glad I filled it in. I could never be a 'yes', 'no', 'sometimes' kind of filler like some of the children in your experiment. When we read your very late letter Mum laughed at the part where you put my answers were 'detailed and delightful'. She said, 'Yeah, just a bit!' I think she was referring to the Lemon Crunch Pie episode but as I said to her, she is always telling me that if a job's worth doing, it's worth doing properly. She rolled her eyes at that and got the ironing out. I like growing up because you can argue with your parents and sometimes win, as long as they like your attitude. If they don't like your attitude, it's best just to go and watch TV.

I thought your results were very interesting and will look good in either bar charts or pie charts done on a high quality colour printer. I feel sorry for the three pupils who have not settled in to Year Seven, unless one of them is Anthony Bent, then I'm only sorry for two of them. Do they go to Bartock High? I'd hate it if they did and I passed them in the corridor or lunch queue every day without knowing. I discussed it with Tamla and she said we could write to them if you gave them our address. Please be quick, though, because there's only a few weeks left before they turn into Year Eights and then anything could happen.

I wish I hadn't mentioned having nothing to write about in Diary 2 now because there's loads going on at the moment, not so much at Mum's as at Dad's and I'm allowed to write about Dad's. Do you remember when Alexis was helping Toni because her life was going nowhere? Well, they went to a spiritualist called Mrs Pitchfork for guidance and Mrs Pitchfork told them that their fortunes lay in transforming others so they're opening a fancy dress hire shop in Dad's stockroom. All they need is funding and somewhere to put the cough candy. I'm not sure what Dad's opinion is but Alexis has moved her exercise bike back in so that's a sign that Dad's fathoming women again. Mel and me can't wait to try on the costumes when they arrive. We can play *Stars in Your Eyes* after closing time.

Anyway, if you change your mind or if Professor Shingle tells you he wants more diaries from us, I suggest you pick July 17th–21st—Activities Week. During Activities Week there are no lessons and all the teachers relax and wear casual clothing while experts take over. I bet even the 'yes', 'no', 'sometimes' lot would find plenty to write about because Activities Week has something for everyone.

Most people, like Chloe and Josephine, chose the trips to Disneyland Paris and Alton Towers because that's where their boyfriends chose (yawn, yawn). Their boyfriends are Year Nines and smell of Lynx but I don't know much else about them, mainly because I haven't asked. Chloe would only tell me more than I want to know.

Clifford and Peter are going camping near Wooky Hole with Mr Kanchelsis and Mrs Warrener. You wouldn't recognize Clifford now, Mr Cohen, he's so different since Mrs Bacon became his temporary foster carer after the eviction. He's still an elective mute but he smiles and nods more and has cut right down on his detentions and flapjack buying.

Tamla's writing a book from Monday to Wednesday and doing drama with Jem on Thursday and Friday. He's been brought in to run specialist workshops for the keen and interested. I am keen and interested but could not resist a **whole week** in the CDT rooms with Mr O'Connell. Jem understands and says you have to follow your heart. Tamla understands, too. It's a relief having a friend who is fine about letting you do your own thing and doesn't go into a mardy if you show independence.

Only Anthony isn't participating in Activities Week. He's having private tuition instead. Ever since Mrs Ruskin told Mr and Mrs Bent at parents' evening he could take maths GCSE tomorrow and get an A star he's been a mega swell-head. Mrs Bent should be careful or her son's brain will explode all over her kitchen units one of these days and all that swotting will have been wasted. I think Mrs Bent should give her son a break and concentrate on her own class instead. They're going through the *sixes and sevens*, worrying about starting secondary, like I did this time last year.

Melanie's getting really wound up about it. I showed her your statistics but she said they didn't really mean anything to her and nothing I said helped so I wrote her a poem. It could be for any Year Sixes, really. I showed it to Mr Pikelet first so he could check the metre (not the gas meter, in case you crack bad jokes like my dad). Mr Pikelet thought it was *inspirational* and showed it to Mrs Warrener and Mrs Warrener asked if she could read it out to all the Year Sixes on her class visits so I said she could if Melanie agreed. Melanie did agree as long as nobody mentioned her name in case everybody stared at her on her first day at Bartock High, so the poem has two titles like Shakespeare's stuff. When Chloe read the poem she said, 'I suppose the verse about "fakes" means me', and I said, 'If you say so', and she grinned. That's how we are with each other now. Not exactly friends but not exactly enemies.

Anyway, here's the poem.

# Melanie's Poem
## Or
# A Poem for Year Sixes about to start Year Seven

Don't be worried
Don't be scared
The teachers are fine
Ignore what you've heard

Don't be mean
Don't be passive
You'll like the school
Although it's massive

The dinners are great
The flapjacks are ace
Ignore the Year Eights
If they push in your place

Do your homework
Fill in your planners
The teachers are nice
But keen on good manners

There are hundreds of pupils
Who'll make proper mates
If your old ones dump you
Or turn into fakes

There are discos and clubs
Trips to go bowling
Year Seven is ace
There's no need for moaning

At home life will change
That's also a fact
They'll nag about homework
And *is your bag packed*?

If, like me,
You live in two houses
Have double of everything
Like knickers and blouses

Your hair will go greasy
After, like, one hour
Your armpits will pong
You'll need a shower

What more can I say
To you Year Sixes
Just go for it kids
And be good mixers

I know it's not a classic but it is based on truth and experience and that's what counts.

Is Gareth going to throw you a massive party when you get your MA? I think he should because it's a real achievement. Jem and I are planning a party for my mum when she finishes her diploma next year. That's *if* she finishes it. She's already two essays behind because she keeps throwing up. I asked her if she was in the early stages of pregnancy but she told me not to be ridiculous, it was just a bug going round. It must be a grumpy bug, that's all I can say.

Good luck with your collating, Mr Cohen.
Shalom!

Your best form filler

*Simone Anna Wibberley*

Simone Anna Wibberley

# Announcement

### Thanks

I would like to send out a personal thanks to all the staff and pupils of Woodhill Primary, John Blow Primary, Bartock High, Tuxford Comprehensive, and Robert Pattinson Comprehensive who helped me in my research last year. A special thanks to Simone, Anthony, Freddie, Joe P, Joe J-W, Avril, Tim, Molly, Harry B, Hilary, Hannah, Jessica, Simon, Sarah, Woody, Josephine, Laura DV, Connor, Michael, Will, Elinor, Timmy, Christie, Paddy, Claudia, Louisa, Tilly, Dhani, and Oscar.

I couldn't have done it without you.

And finally to Gareth, who supported me all the way through.

Ben Cohen MA

# Other books by Helena Pielichaty

## Simone's Letters

ISBN 0 19 275087 9

*Dear Mr Cakebread ... For starters my name is Simone, not Simon ... Mum says you sound just like my dad. My dad, Dennis, lives in Bartock with his girlfriend, Alexis ... My mum says lots of rude things about her because Alexis was one of the reasons my parents got divorced (I was the other) ...*

When ten-year-old Simone starts writing letters to Jem Cakebread, the leading man of a touring theatre company, she begins a friendship that will change her life ... and the lives of all around her: her mum, her best friend Chole, her new friend Melanie – and not forgetting Jem himself!

This collection of funny and often touching letters charts Simone's final year at Primary School; from a school visit to *Rumpelstiltskin's Revenge* to her final leaving Assembly; through the ups and downs of her friendships – and those of her mum and dad.

## Jade's Story

ISBN 0 19 271841 X

What do you do when your dad starts behaving oddly? When he just sits in a chair all day, staring into space, and you get too embarrassed to bring your friends home? And what about when he finally flips and makes a scene in the middle of the road and has to be carted off to hospital? You want to talk to your mum about it, but she's too busy worrying about your dad. You're scared that no one will understand and you think your dad doesn't love you any more.

This is what happened to Jade one summer. This is the story of how she coped. It's a story of secrets and of discovery. It's Jade's story.

# Vicious Circle

ISBN 0 19 275113 1

*Why haven't we got any money? We've never got any money.*
*Why can't we be like other people and have fish and chips when we fancy?'*

Ten-year-old Louisa May and her mother Georgette are two of the 'have-nots', shuttling between ever-seedier bed and breakfast accommodation. To help cope with this way of life they play elaborate fantasy games, pretending to be the characters in the romantic fiction that Georgette borrows from the library in every town they move to.

When they arrive at the Cliff Top Villas Hotel in a run-down seaside resort and Georgette falls ill, it looks as if the fantasy will have to end. But Louisa May enlists the help of Joanna, another hotel resident, and together they determine to find out the truth behind Georgette's 'let's pretend' existence. Maybe this way there will be a chance for them to break out of the vicious circle and become 'haves' at last ...

# Getting Rid of Karenna

ISBN 0 19 271819 3

*It was happening again and I felt as hopeless and stupid as ever. When you were scared, you were scared and nothing could take away that sick, twisted feeling you got in the pit of your stomach, no matter how old you were.*

Even now Suzanne can remember the fear, the humiliation, the pain, caused by the constant bullying; the two year reign of terror in which she had been driven to the brink of a breakdown. It is three years since Karenna left the school and Suzanne is beginning to put it all behind her, but suddenly Karenna has come back into her life. Is it all going to begin again? Will she never be free of the nightmare? In order to get on with her own life, Suzanne has to find some way to rid herself of the past ... of Karenna.